JUST A TOY

BY GINA AND MERCER MAYER

*To Caleb
and Justine McNair
with love.*

A GOLDEN BOOK • NEW YORK

Golden Books Publishing Company, Inc., New York, New York 10106

Just A Toy book, characters, text, and images © 2000 Gina and Mercer Mayer. LITTLE CRITTER, MERCER MAYER'S LITTLE CRITTER, and MERCER MAYER'S LITTLE CRITTER Logo are registered trademarks of Orchard House Licensing Company. All rights reserved. Printed in the U.S.A. No part of this book may be reproduced or copied in any form without written permission from the copyright owner. GOLDEN BOOKS®, A GOLDEN BOOK®, A GOLDEN STORYBOOK™, G DESIGN®, and the distinctive gold spine are trademarks of Golden Books Publishing Company, Inc. Library of Congress Catalog Card Number: 99-67483
ISBN: 0-307-13279-X   A MM   First Edition 2000

Dad took my sister and me to the toy store. We had been extra helpful to mom all week so this was our treat.

We went to TOYS EVERYWHERE—
and they were everywhere. I was amazed.

My sister went right up to the science section
and picked out a microscope or something.

Boy, is she easy to please. I just couldn't make up my mind.

First I wanted a whirring, zooming, flashing spaceship with a parachute.

Then I saw the Rough 'n' Ready Smasher Truck.

AWESOME!

NEW!

WOW

But I had always wanted a Mr. Build Me Set.

Then I saw the Roaring,
Stomping, Hopping Dinosaur.

HEAR ME ROAR!
WATCH ME STOMP!
SEE ME HOP!

Dad said, "Time to make up your mind."
But I couldn't make up my mind. I was confused.
Finally, I picked the whirring, zooming, flashing
spaceship with a parachute.

We stood in line. But just as it was our turn at the cashier, I knew for sure that I didn't want the whirring, zooming, flashing spaceship with a parachute. I wanted the Roaring, Stomping, Hopping Dinosaur.

"Dad, Dad!" I said. "We made a terrible mistake. I got the wrong toy."

Dad and my little sister didn't look
very happy, but we went back and got
the dinosaur.

We had to stand in line all over again.
Dad paid and we went to the car. I was
happy and my little sister was happy.

But on the way home my dinosaur's head fell off. I started to cry. Dad said, "Don't worry, I can fix it."

My little sister started collecting things to look at under her dumb microscope. I had to wait for Dad to fix my dinosaur.

Finally, it was fixed. I thought I would fool my sister, so I set my dinosaur on its loudest roar and snuck up behind her. But my dinosaur didn't roar. It just squeaked. She laughed.

Then I made it stomp real hard and it fell all to pieces.
My sister laughed some more. I cried.

Mom said, "Don't worry. Dad can fix it."

I guess I threw a fit. I screamed, "I don't want a fixed
toy. I want a new, unbroken toy, now!"

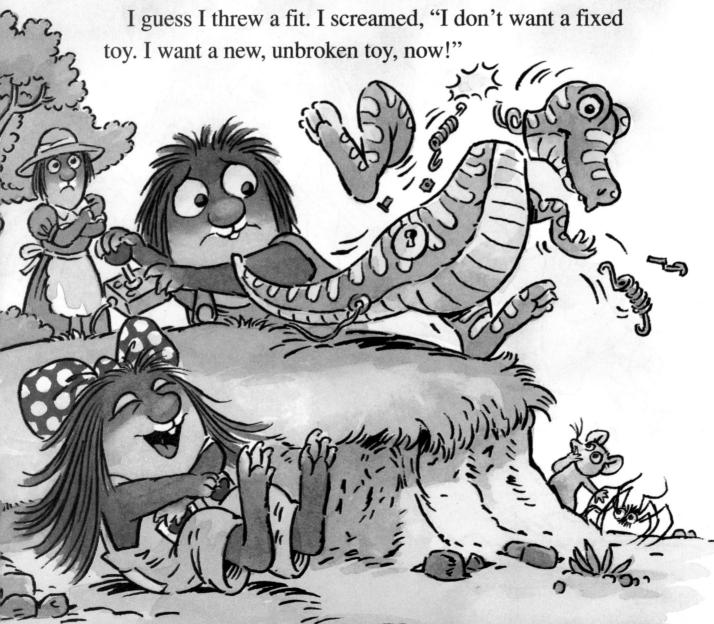

Mom sent me to my room until dinner.

At dinner I had to say I was sorry to everyone. Then Mom said that tomorrow Dad would take me back to the toy store for an exchange.

The next day I had to wait all day long for Dad to get home from work. It was the longest day of my life.

Dad took me and my broken dinosaur to the toy store. We went to the return counter and the lady gave me a slip.

I got the Mr. Build Me Set. It's already in
billions of pieces so there's nothing to break.

Dad said, "Now do you feel better?
After all, it's just a toy."
I said, "Yeah, Dad, but it's a great toy!"